Alone in Exile

Alone in Exile

Iridescent Toad Publishing

Iridescent Toad Publishing.

Book cover by Lily Dormishev.

First edition. ISBN: 978-1-9163478-5-4

*Extra special thanks to Des M. Astor
for helping me bring this book to life.*

Prologue

"She's beautiful," a gentle feminine voice purred.

"Indeed," replied a deep masculine voice. "She has your eyes, my love."

The woman traced a delicate nail through the newborn's soft hair. The man's arm was draped over the woman, his pale black-clawed hand on her shoulder.

The unusual couple stared in adoration at the new member of their family. Ada Tepez was freshly bathed and resting in her mother's arms. With her brilliant blue eyes partially closed, she gently suckled milk from her mother. The child had a few beauty marks on her pale skin, but otherwise was without any other blemishes or complications from birth.

The cold season was closing in rapidly, and so the newborn was wrapped up warm in various furs that the couple had prepared in advance. They knew how to hunt.

A few candles on side tables illuminated the room as the last rays of the dying sun faded into a starlit night. Rather than create an eerie environment, the lighting made everything cosy.

The child's father – a male vampire with slicked-back hair and deep crimson eyes – bent forward to plant a gentle kiss on his wife's forehead. A happy smile played on his lips, showing the slightest hint of fang. Ada's mother took notice of this and raised her eyebrow curiously.

"Hmm… Do you think she will have your teeth, my love? Or perhaps require blood soon?" she asked, deep in thought.

There were a few puncture wounds on the woman's neck, indicating love bites, of course. The vampire shook his head, tapping a claw upon his chin after leaning back a tad.

"She won't be able to access her powers without the blood. However, she will not require them. We will keep her safe. She can sustain on human food – that I promise. There is no need to worry," he said.

His confidence enabled the mother to relax somewhat.

"Wonderful," she said.

She had breathed the words blissfully before staring at her lover expectantly.

"You need to rest," he said. "I will have breakfast prepared for you when you wake up. How does that sound?"

She gave a nod of agreement. With that, he left for a little while to do some organising and cleaning, eventually transitioning to cooking.

This was a far cry from raging war on mortals. He much preferred it. The mundane activities were a testament to his established humanity – something that the vampire was extremely grateful to his lover for. All the same, he could not help but worry every so often that his past might catch up with him someday. Still, he pushed those thoughts aside. The new family had much to do, and dwelling would only be detrimental.

Leaving his wife and child to rest, he wandered through a relatively small wooden house that had just a few rooms. He kindled the wood stove, content that it would heat up the house. The chilly season was evident by the changing leaves outside. The furs around the house would only do so much to provide warmth.

He looked out of the window as the cloak of darkness thickened outside. A blanket of stars lit up the night sky; it was beautiful but indicative of the need to light more candles. As the house warmed up, he did so too, ensuring to do some more cleaning along the way.

He moved past various pieces of art on the wall; landscapes depicting faraway scenes such as rolling fields of grass, and forests that seemed to stretch forever. All places he'd travelled and painted himself at one point.

Upon finishing his chores, the vampire returned to his lover's bedside. Along with their child, she had been asleep for a few hours whilst he'd worked. It had afforded him the chance to prepare a hearty breakfast of eggs. He'd managed to get them from the market just a day prior, fresh from the farmer.

The woman's glimmering green eyes fixed on him, a soft smile on her lips. She accepted the plate and shifted over as he climbed into the bed to sit next to her. They snuggled up together, gazing in adoration at their child. The scent of warm wax and woodsmoke flowed through the air, further relaxing the exhausted mother.

"Little Ada," the human woman cooed.

She gently wiggled her finger to allow the baby to grasp it. Although it wasn't unusual for a newborn to have such a naturally tight grip, Ada's strength was immense. The mother raised an eyebrow and watched as the baby drifted back to sleep, giving a few hiccups before relaxing entirely.

The woman cuddled up even closer to her lover and let out a soft sigh.

"We have enough furs for the winter season, right? Along with many salted meats?" she asked.

She was met with a serious nod from the vampire.

"Yes," he said. "Along with the herbs rumoured to have magical properties. They will do well for any ailments that may come up. Hopefully we won't need them."

Satisfied, the woman allowed her shoulders to slump.

"Excellent," she said. "I managed to get a wool blanket from the marketplace. It will do well in keeping her warm."

And keep her warm it did. Other than when the family had a mild scare with a tiny cold, the winter passed without complication. The wood stove heated the house well – with the furs and blankets taking care of the rest. Before the family knew it, spring had arrived, and with it, new beginnings.

Ada hadn't been outside much before. Her curious glimmering eyes followed the birds that flew around and landed on the branches of the trees. Taking a walk outside to the nearby forest, the mother carried baby Ada in her arms. Ada's father strolled along with them. He was dressed in simple clothing. He'd passed up the elegance of what he used to wear shortly after he and his human lover had met.

In his gloved hand was a parasol, shielding his "sensitive skin" from the sun. Due to his power, he wouldn't burst into flames upon the rays touching him, but would certainly be scalded within ten minutes should they linger on him for too long. The accessory aided in protecting him from that, as did the shade from the trees when the family entered the forest.

Ada lifted her little arms, grasping at the air in front of her when she spotted a tiny songbird flying across the sky. She let out several coos and gurgles, unable to actually snatch the birds up, but perhaps wishing that she could. This prompted her father to chuckle. He lovingly bent down and brushed his nose up against hers, shaking his head delicately back and forth for some "nose kisses". Keeling giggles of delight spilled from the child, and soon the entire family lost themselves in the joy of the laughter.

"What a beautiful day this is," Ada's mother said happily.

She sat down on a log, taking care not to sit on any bugs. Her lover sat beside her, leaning against her and withdrawing a book from his woven bag. The cover was weathered and the paper was somewhat wrinkled, but he would be able to read it all the same.

"Indeed," he said. "I admit to being grateful that winter was only mild. Ada had that cough and sniffle to get through, but look at how her eyes shine now."

Indeed, the baby's expression gleamed with enthusiasm as she continued to try and grasp at everything in and out of range. Her mother began to occupy her by playing, grabbing her husband's bag and pulling out a little sheep cuddly toy for her to hold.

The family took their opportunity to enjoy this beautiful day, turning in when dusk approached. The vampire was practically turning diurnal from this activity! He didn't mind though. His thoughts turned to how much he'd mellowed and relaxed since growing his family. Ada hadn't been planned but she was a light in his life that grounded him further.

Despite enjoying the stabilities and comforts of family life, it was hard for him to ignore the whispers and bitter voices that he would sometimes hear when wandering along the cobblestone roads of the town. *Surely nobody knows of my secret?* he pondered. He'd left that life behind long ago, and had very specific targets for his bloodlust now. The innocent no longer suffered under his fangs. So why, therefore, did he sometimes have a horrible feeling that something awful was about to happen?

He refocused his attention to his wife and child, telling himself to shove those thoughts down well. They were home now and it was not the time to be morbid. Ada's mother settled in, changing the baby and cleaning her up with a nice bath that had been prepared by the warmth of the stove. When this was finished, the vampire dumped the water, planning on boiling some again tomorrow in preparation for a few days' time.

Now the baby's scent was fresh and clean, her hair still wet as she began to nurse once more. Ada was mercifully a mild baby, never one to cry too much – only if she was displeased to the maximum degree, which did not happen often. There was not much in the small house, but it was just enough for the family to live on happily.

Since this was feeding night, after ensuring his wife and child were safe, the male vampire left in the form of a bat. He had been keeping an ear out for the riffraff of the town and had realised that the local drunkard had been going too far with his unacceptable behaviour. To the point where, rumour had it, he'd dragged off an inebriated woman against her will.

Mr Tepez landed in the shadows of a wooden house, the dirt road beaten down by the hooves of various animals that always passed on through. The stench of human sweat and body odour led him to his target: the drunk in ripped rags who had passed out in a corner.

The vampire sneered, glad for the opportunity to rid the world of such filth. With his inhuman speed, he lunged at the man. He ripped into his neck. Blood began to spray before any scream could escape. The vampire gorged upon the sweet crimson liquid, memories flashing through his mind.

The villagers running and screaming as the monster cut them down, remorseless, keeling with dark laughter and the promise of death. So many corpses, none spared; not innocent men, women, or children. The vampire was the scourge on so many villages. Would this carnage ever stop?

A shudder went through the vampire's spine as he dropped the corpse, allowing the limp body to flop against the ground, sending up a puff of dust. He'd had his fill, his fangs dripping with delicious blood. His mood had soured after that thought though. He'd worked so hard to change, yet those images reminded him every so often of his past.

He sighed and endeavoured to breathe calmly. His eyes fell upon the lifeless corpse, something he'd ripped into so easily. Doubt filled his soul, but there was no way that *this* town would find out. They would blame it on the wolves. They always did.

A soft red glow covered the concerned vampire as he shifted into a bat. He flew towards the glimmering stars. Not a cloud was in the sky as he made his way back home, well fed. His mood would brighten significantly upon being able to rest with his family. His lover had tempered his devilish ways, and he would stay that way forevermore. He would protect dear Ada from *his* harsh reality. She would not make the same mistakes that he foolishly had.

When he entered the small home, he walked past several candles that were due to flicker out. He wandered into the room and changed out of his hunting clothes, replacing them with lighter material for sleep. Finally, he got himself into bed, leaving a soft kiss upon Ada's head as she slept next to her mother. Groggily did his wife turn her head and give him a smile.

"Everything alright?" she asked.

"Yes, of course, my darling," he said, his voice betraying the lie.

The woman did not press. She knew it was a topic that tore at him. It didn't cross his mind every time he fed, and was becoming less frequent, but the trauma of his past was difficult to leave behind.

"Rest with me and relax your mind," she said finally.

And that he did.

He knew deep down that he could not fly away from his past entirely. Baby Ada, however, would be spared from that madness. She would not be brought down by his mistakes. He was sure of it.

Right?

Chapter One

Run... RUN!

Ada was doing all in her power to escape them, but they drew ever closer as her lungs burned. It was like the tales in her books; mobs running monsters down and ripping them apart – only this was her reality. They brandished pitchforks and torches, screaming into the night, growing closer and closer.

"Death to the monster! DEATH TO THE MONSTER!" several voices shouted.

Ada needed to find a place to hide, and fast. Her moon-white hair blew back in the wind as she ran. She was dressed in a variety of simple loose fabrics. They had been dyed with deeper colours. They flowed against the breeze, just like her hair.

Her chest heaved as she carried onwards, desperate

to get away. Luckily she'd been keeping herself in good shape over the past couple of decades. She'd learned to be a hunter in the family, often able to chase down rabbits without complication. That helped her here, where unfortunately, she was now the prey.

The cries of the baying hounds hit her ears, causing her to wince and whimper. Her gleaming sapphire eyes nearly reflected the moon's light, but not quite. That hadn't given her away over all these years, but her father's past had. She had to push those *images* to the back of her mind. Right now, her goal was survival.

Pines whisked past, needles reminding her of the daggers the mob held. Along with other tools, they were no doubt intended to lacerate her skin and bleed her dry. She would not let the mob get to that point; she would survive them against all odds.

Mercifully, the barking and yelling began to fade slightly as she progressed deeper into the forest. She pushed aside the worry of monstrous legends for a moment, needing to find a safe place to hide. A cave wouldn't do – the dogs would surely chase her into it. She couldn't just climb up into a tree though, for they would wait beneath it.

She needed to stop and rest for a moment to gather her thoughts. Time was of the essence, but collapsing in exhaustion would not do. A squirrel darted along a branch overhead, pausing to curiously stare her down before moving on. The eerie peace of the wildlife caused her stomach to clench, worsening the sick feeling she already had billowing in her gut. Why couldn't things have remained serene at her hometown?

Composing herself, she began to run once more. The dangerous shouts of the townsfolk were on the rise again. She needed to think fast. Several strands of her hair fell into her face as she carried on, looking for someplace – *any place* – where she could get away without being flayed or burned.

Luckily, the sound of flowing water hit her ears, causing her to exhale sharply. She ran towards the moon, which soon enough reflected off of a river. *Thank God.* With just one determined leap into the water, her clothing was immediately soaked. The bone-chilling temperature hit her entire body as the current tugged at her, trying to pull her under.

She was a strong swimmer. The weight of her clothing did little to slow her down. Her muscles rippled as she stayed on the surface. She knew she had very little time before the mob could catch her up. Even if she had been pulling ahead for a little while, that advantage would certainly not last forever.

In the process of swimming to the other side, she had taken in several gulps of water. She threw herself on the shore and erupted into a choking fit. She clawed at her throat with her slightly chipped nails, coughing up water and willing herself not to feel dizzy. She took a minute or so to get ahold of herself before she could run again. Knowing that the townsfolk could find a bridge upriver, she'd avoided such an obvious route and had also managed to wash her scent away. All things considered, she had got to the other side at speed.

They would not relent though, she knew as much. They'd searched for *years* to eradicate her loved ones. Tears began to spill down her cheeks, a wave of emotion bombarding her. She wasn't safe from the danger yet. She had to keep moving.

Still running, Ada Tepez bent down to collect some pine needles as she darted swiftly past more trees. Along with other scents like wildflowers and mud, she rubbed them over her skin and clothes. Hopefully this would be enough. She was light enough on her feet and wouldn't leave very many discernable tracks – at least not ones that could be easily seen until daytime.

With that, she reached up into a tree, using her upper body strength to pull herself up, branch by branch. Once she'd got to the thickest part of the tree, she allowed herself to pause. The only sound in the distance was that of the roaring river, which she'd left behind quite a while ago, at least. She shuddered as a cold breeze rushed against her skin. It reminded her that winter was going to set in soon, and that she would be vulnerable to the elements.

The little scratches she'd obtained in the process of settling into the tree were nothing compared to the other wounds she'd suffered when the baying mob had initially attacked her home. The scent of smoke still clung to her clothing, and the deep sting of everything – physically and emotionally – triggered more tears to drip down her cheeks.

She started to rip and tug her clothing into practical rags. Whilst not removing them entirely, it was an opportunity to inspect her wounds. There were deep red welts on her flesh, and burns from when her house had been set on fire. She'd lost everything. The townsfolk had managed to land a few blows on her with their pitchforks; there were more than a few lines of oozing puncture marks all over her.

She sniffled, wiping her nose with the back of her hand. She pressed a few patches of her ripped clothing onto the wounds to stop the bleeding, conscious that she needed to keep her scent hidden. Those relentless monsters would use their hounds to sniff her out – if not tonight, then tomorrow or soon after.

Exhaustion clamped its jaws upon her. She shuddered and closed her eyes. Just a wink or two of sleep was all she needed, really. Then she would be on the move again. Fighting for her life wasn't an easy task, despite her history of being a strong hunter.

As everything faded into the dark, her dreams reminded her of the death of everything she held dear.

Everything had happened so quickly. A bright burst of light, and suddenly, everything was on fire. Ada's father knew that their time was up, but he wasn't about to let his daughter die. Despite how Ada begged to be allowed to stay in hopes of being able to reason with the angry townsfolk – or fight them if they were beyond that – her parents insisted on staying back to buy her a bit more time.

They screamed at her to run and not look back. She didn't listen to them. She crawled out of the window, her skin ripping against the shattered glass. As she looked back over her shoulder, it was to a sight of true horror.

Her father was impaled by several pitchforks, blood pooling beneath him, staining his clothing. His face was contorted in pain, his mouth set open to flash his fangs as he was slain. Blood poured down his chin, dripping to form a puddle on the floor. A wooden stake was brought forward and shoved into his chest, leading to a slow, agonising death.

Tears of blood poured down his cheeks as he thrashed and tried to get away, putting up a fight at the very least before being eradicated. The vampire was vastly outnumbered by the hysterical mob. He was out of practice in using his potent powers, having turned his back on them decades ago. Still, he was able to lash out and rip the eyes from one of the townsfolk – a sweet but short-lived revenge as he expired. His limp body dissolving into ash was the last thing Ada saw of him.

"BURN THE WITCH!"

Her mother suffered an even grislier fate. She was tied to a piece of furniture by twine. The mob used their torches to set her on fire. The scent of burning flesh billowed through the air. Screams of agony from the woman who'd loved Ada so dearly assaulted her senses along with the roaring fire.

At least, in the chaos, a couple of the townsfolk fell to the flames as well. Enough of them would escape though. They were like roaches; numerous, and hard to kill. Where one fell, another took their place.

Ada felt her stomach clench. Once she'd jumped clear of the window, she emptied the contents of her gut upon the ground.

She was dizzy and nauseous, but the evil glares from the eyes of the crowd told her one thing: she was next.

Ada woke with a start, shuddering and moving clumped strands of hair from her face. She took in several gulping breaths as she looked to the sky. It was still dark. She wasn't sure how long she'd been asleep for. Not long enough, that was for sure. She massaged her temples for a bit, letting out several breaths.

She was relieved to notice that her bleeding had stopped. She began to climb down from the tree, wincing at the deep ache that had settled in throughout her body. Not only did she have surface wounds, but she'd overworked herself significantly with the initial run. She rubbed her eyes upon reaching the roots of the tree, keen to think straight and come up with a plan. She had knowledge of this area, so could find some berries to hold herself over for a while if necessary.

Her thoughts were cut short by a snarl from the bushes. She spun around quickly. In front of her was a Romanian hound. The dog had bristling tanned fur and an evil onyx gaze – practically glowing in the night with the desire for Ada's blood.

She let out a shriek as the canine launched itself at her, sinking its teeth into her arm and holding on for a moment. As blood spurted out of the wound, she managed to use her free hand to grab the hound by the scruff of the neck, and rip it off. In an act of panic, her normally blue eyes shifted to a deep blood red.

The hound was sent slamming into a pitchfork-wielding man who had nearly caught up with Ada. Aside from getting tangled with one another, neither the hound nor the human were harmed too greatly, despite how much Ada *hated* them for what they had done.

Off she went again. In her state of panic she was faster than before. Her inhuman powers caused some clawing in her stomach, a feeling she recognised. Bloodlust. Although the feeling was familiar, it wasn't one she'd had to deal with often in her two decades of life. With the guidance of her father, she'd managed to control it. Consequently it had only occurred in times of extreme stress… like now.

Ignoring the bloodlust could cause a frenzy, but there was nothing she could do about it for now. She needed to keep *going.* Her body would consume even more of her precious energy to heal the dog bite. It would stop the bleeding but would cause the gnawing feeling to increase.

The townsfolk were not about to relent. Ada launched back into the shadows of the forest, refusing to go down now. Her emotions were in complete turmoil, though there was one primarily clamping its jaws upon her: fear. She needed to be brave though. She couldn't let her parents' sacrifice be for nothing.

Her ears rang with the frantic voices that screamed behind her.

"FIND THE FREAK! KILL IT!"

Chapter Two

The baying hounds prompted Ada to run faster. She tapped into her inhuman powers to do so. With every step, that damned *gnawing* clawed even harder – until her vision began to shift. Suddenly, she could see more, but it was slightly out of focus. Her pupils had grown to cover her eyes completely, swallowing them in darkness.

Flashes of what she'd gone through stabbed at her mind, causing the fear to shift into anger. Ada couldn't afford to make a bad decision though. She had to keep running. For now.

It wasn't long before she had to slow down and rest against a tree. She'd outpaced the humans and their hounds briefly, but her chest was still heaving. She was running low on energy. Once more, she began to rub mud and nearby herbs all over her, applying pressures to at least stop the bleeding. Hopefully the scents would be enough to hide her from the dogs. The screams of humans and the barking from the hounds were fading into the distance, branching off in various directions; the mob had probably divided into groups to look for her.

Sadly, Ada was unlucky. It happened so fast. A hound found her. It darted from the bushes and latched onto her arm, exactly where the last dog's bite was. Ada shrieked, and then into her shoulder slammed three sharp pikes from the edge of a pitchfork. Her eyes stared into those of a man who had lost all humanity and reasoning. A cruel smile twisted across his face.

"Caught the final monster," he said in a gritty tone. "Yer death will be slow. Never done one of them in before. Might as well have some fun with it."

Ada understood the implication, and it was in this moment of clarity that she called upon the darkest parts of her soul. She didn't need to hold back. It was now or never. Suddenly, she used her other hand and scruffed the hound. She threw it away from her with an abundance of strength. It hit the ground with a yelp. Taken by fear, it tore away with a frantic limp, whimpering and rightfully abandoning its master.

Ada's eyes fell upon the man. She smiled lightly before wrapping her hand around the connecting point of the pitchfork. She ripped it out of her shoulder, ignoring the blood that began to drip from her wound. Giving a guttural inhuman snarl, her pitch-black gaze latched on to the man's now-terrified eyes.

"You have made a mistake," she said plainly.

She threw the pitchfork aside so hard that it cracked at its base against a tree, leaving a deep divot. Without delay, she was upon the man. Her teeth, which had sharpened into fangs, ripped into his throat as her nails morphed into claws.

Flesh tore and blood covered her. She didn't care. She had *never* fed from a human before, not like this. Driven to the point of frenzy though, she could not stop. She ripped the flesh open from his chest, snapping his ribs open and reaching for his heart. He was limp now. He'd stopped struggling when he'd choked on his own blood.

From there, she claimed his heart, tearing into the meat like a hungered wolf. Power surged through her veins, so potent that she nearly let out a drunken laugh. As the sound of more people drew closer though, she calmed down from the ecstasy of feeding – able to realise that she needed to move. *Now.*

After a brief period of time as the wind howled bitterly around her, she found a tiny cave. It was barely large enough to accommodate her slim body. Its entrance was covered by a thick bush, and she had to fight the thorns to actually get inside. Once she had, her breath caught as the rustling of footsteps drew closer.

A tear crawled down Ada's cheek as the loud wet sound of sniffing hit her ears, indicating that the hounds had found her. Surprisingly though, she heard a whimper from one nearby and a shuffling sound as it bounded away. Several voices rose up in question, but the hounds didn't lead their masters to her. They sensed something violent and dangerous hiding there, beyond what they were used to dealing with. They would have no chance in a fight to the death.

There was even a point at which the sound of heavy footsteps was terrifyingly close. She closed her eyes, counting slowly as she heard the steps halt right in front of her. A gruff tone rang out.

"How could you lose her scent?!"

"I think she went a different way," another one of the townsfolk replied. "The hounds ain't indicating any sign of the monster here."

"You hear that yelling?! What are they shouting about?!" the first man snarled.

And off the two men went. Ada let out a sigh of relief. Perhaps it *was* that odd change in her when she'd snapped that had frightened the other hounds away; just like it had for the first one that had limped off prior to her ripping its master apart. Whatever the reason, she thanked her lucky stars and waited until the sound of footsteps had faded into the distance.

Ada imagined they would stumble upon the corpse of the man she'd ripped apart. She didn't feel any remorse. She searched within herself to try and figure out why this could be, and realised that for her too, it had been a matter of life or death. He'd also threatened various types of torture – something that had caused her stomach to turn. She decided not to dwell on or feel guilty over what she had done. Not for now, at least. It might come up later, but it would not do her well to become consumed with it at this moment in time.

The burst of energy she'd obtained from her feeding was quickly fading. Her body had used it to heal her deep wounds. She was covered in her own blood, which was now drying and caked on her skin. Desperate for even just some respite, it was the least of her concerns.

A cold breeze billowed into the cave, sending shivers down her spine. She stared out towards the opening with narrowed eyes as the first rays of sun greeted the world. The sun wasn't a threat to her but she had always been nocturnal, mostly anyway. She wanted to sleep but knew it was too dangerous for that.

It didn't matter one bit. She soon found herself fading away. The tiny amount of sleep she'd managed to grasp whilst in the tree hadn't been sufficient. She'd fought the exhaustion as much as she could, but in the end, it won out.

Bombarded with nightmares, Ada awoke several times during the day, her chest heaving. She managed to make it through until dusk though, where she would need to continue pulling through.

***

The stars shone above as the breeze swept through, cold and unforgiving. Ada shivered, knowing that the approaching winter would be relentless. With no home to return to and with no food, she had no idea what her future would look like. She buried her face into her hands, sobbing softly for a while, unable to help it. She kept getting hit again and again with reality; this was the opposite of something she could handle well.

But she had to.

You're a hunter, Ada. You need to keep going, she told herself, taking several deep breaths. She fixed her gaze upon the bush in front of the small cave, gaining the courage to suffer the ripping thorns once more. Her skin would knit itself back together, though significantly more slowly than it had done after she'd slain that man.

Strangely, she was no longer plagued by that odd gnawing feeling that had overcome her when she'd charged from the mob. She felt regular hunger now – its claws from a different beast, but a beast all the same. She would need to satisfy that at some point. First though, she would need to get away from this area entirely, as it was too dangerous.

She wandered through the forest. She was extremely jumpy, her head turning every so often at various rustlings from the trees. Nearly every muscle in her body was tense from the stress, and she couldn't get rid of the fear that clenched her stomach. Still, she increased her pace, reassured by the moon and mellow weather.

Mellow for now anyway. There were some clouds gathering above, telling her that she would do well to move on quickly and find shelter somewhere. She stepped out of the forest and onto some rolling fields, the grass brushing against her damaged legs. The ripped clothing that hung from her body exposed them abundantly. She continued to run across the field, stopping to catch her breath every so often.

Several hours later, Ada found herself in a new forest. The town was long behind her. She was thankful for this but was very aware of how she had no belongings and no means with which to sustain herself, aside from her intelligence. Thus, she began to forage, collecting various edible plants and the very few berries that had managed to survive the weather getting colder and colder.

Another few hours passed and she'd managed to gather some wood and start a fire. That had eaten up quite a bit of her energy, but the warmth would help her tonight. Strangely, the animals of the forest did not bother her, perhaps sensing her nature as well. Ada tried not to think about this as she consumed some of the flora she'd gathered. She started to think about the traps she could set to hunt meat with. She would need the protein.

She found shelter in a large hollowed-out tree. She would begin her hunting tomorrow. Hopefully after that, she'd be able to seek out some sort of town to… well, she was not sure. She stared at her bloodstained hands and realised that she would belong nowhere. Not to mention, what if another town turned on her just like her place of birth had? Word travelled extremely slowly from one town to another, usually carried by nobility or merchants. But it might reach another eventually, especially since the incident had happened in this region. Ada hoped that her habit of shyly hiding her face in town would be a boon of sorts.

Even if her worries were right and even if the odds were truly against her, Ada knew that she couldn't give up now. Her parents had sacrificed valuable time so that she could run free. She was not about to waste that.

Chapter Three

Another fire, another night. Ada warmed her hands, gazing up at the moon and allowing herself to mourn properly. It had been three days since the mob had murdered her parents and chased her out of town. She had been on the move since then. As she'd travelled through the shadows of the forest, the animals of the night had avoided her at all costs. Her aura had changed since she'd feasted upon that man's blood.

She had no urge to repeat such activity. The only strong emotion that swelled over her was one of grief. Off to her side was the limp corpse of a vole. The animal's neck had snapped in the trap she'd set. She silently thanked the creature and began to cook it over the fire, having impaled it upon a sharpened stick.

She then ate slowly, shuddering every other minute and taking a few gasping breaths. Although she felt a deep sadness, she knew that she needed to step up. Her parents would not want her to squander her life away in misery.

Finishing her meal and feeling better for it, she stood up and observed her surroundings. An endless sea of pines greeted her, serene in a way. The stars sparkled above – some peeking out from behind the cover of clouds. The scent of cooked meat was joined with the musky smell of deer and various herbs. The chirps of insects all around reminded her of just how alive this forest was, despite her off-putting aura.

A colony of bats flew above, their chittering far removed from reality down below. Narrowing her gaze, Ada tried to study their gleaming eyes. There was not one glow of red among them. Not that a passing vampire would help anyway. Her father was the only vampire she'd ever known. She had been told to be wary of vampires who were outsiders.

Making a conscious effort to ignore her negative feelings, she calmly sat down to think. The vole meat wouldn't grant her with any powers. The small pool of energy it had provided had now dried up entirely.

Aside from the fact that another town could find out who she was, Ada had no idea where one could even *be. Look to the sky again,* she told herself. Despite what fire had done to her mother, she needed it and was utilising it right now. She vowed to use it to her advantage. She would need to look to the sky at dusk when she travelled. With any luck, she would see smoke rising into the air, indicating a possible nearby town to investigate.

With that, after ample rest, she was on the move again. Although her wounds were on the mend, they still stung quite frequently and reminded her of the true terror she'd left behind. That's why she needed to keep walking – to get caught in a net of thoughts would result in death.

Do I want revenge?

The question was unsettling, and as she walked, her eyes gleamed in thought. She tapped a dirty nail upon her chin, then proceeded to shake her head. Seeking revenge would be pointless. She would allow herself to mourn, but any thoughts of returning and initiating battle were shoved away into the darkest depths of her mind.

Onwards she walked, passing by so many trees, hoping that she was going *somewhere.* She was without an aim, taking shots in the dark and hoping to land upon something – anything. She followed the brightest star, willing herself forwards with each step. Some were harder than others, but she managed.

Ada had lost track of how many nights had passed when she finally collapsed in an area without ample shelter. The winds were growing increasingly frigid, and food was becoming harder to find. Her stomach growled, reminding her that she needed to eat soon. Her skin was rather tight on her bones now. She could feel weakness setting in at an alarming rate.

She had broken through the forest and into another clearing about an hour ago. Too exhausted, she hadn't bothered to find a cave. Instead, she had haphazardly settled in the shade under a tree in a pile of leaves. The bugs didn't bother her now; they hadn't even bothered her in the first place. Despite their annoying presence, they were the least of her concerns. She felt them crawling along her skin, a pinprick every so often to indicate that they were biting her. Not that it mattered; the only thing that did was making it through to another day.

Her half-closed eyes fell upon something rising into the air. *Smoke: a column of it in the distance.* At seeing an indication of the presence of civilisation, Ada felt her heart flutter.

This could be my chance…

She was too weak to go and investigate right now. A day's sleep would do her well and would put her in a better frame of mind to prepare for what to do next. Who was she? A hunter who'd had a bad run-in with a town and had to flee? A noblewoman running away from her kingdom due to corruption? The mistreated farmer's daughter who'd finally decided to do something about it?

All of those stories had their merit, but Ada wasn't sure which would stick the best. She had a *massive* amount of scarring that would not go away, but no one would believe that she was a soldier of any sort. She gulped, hoping that her condition would not lead to suspicion.

***

Dusk arrived. Ada awoke in a cold sweat. Something was wrong. She could not figure out the off-feeling until she suddenly recognised the sound that was drawing closer.

Barking. Of a hound.

"No! No no no!" she screamed.

She scrambled to her feet but immediately fell to the ground. She tried again, successful this time. The murky shadows of dusk were spreading. Hurling herself into the forest, she tore through the trees, hitting her shoulder on a few of them and letting out a cry of agony. The extent of her weakness made itself apparent and she soon found herself stumbling.

Woof! Woof woof woof!

"NO!" Ada screamed.

The dog drew mercilessly closer. Tears prickled Ada's eyes as the images of rabid townsfolk entered her mind, eager to rip her limb from limb. It couldn't end like this!

Evidently, it could, because she simply could not keep running. She collapsed onto the ground, her chest heaving as more tears poured down her face. She resolved to rub her arm and hope that the hound would not catch her. She was granted no such luck.

After some rustling of leaves, a hound burst forth from the underbrush. The animal was the opposite of aggressive. A large wet nose shoved itself into Ada's face as she shrieked in terror. The hound had short black fur with splotches of brown. Its ears flopped as it jumped back, startled by her reaction. The hound then whimpered, tucking its long tail between its legs and lowering its head.

Ada held her head in her hands, covering her face as the hound approached again. The hound then turned and rushed off into the forest, perhaps to leave Ada in peace. Anxious that someone was probably following behind it, Ada tried to get herself to sit up. Exhausted, she fell back down again with a groan.

Much to her dismay, the hound wasn't done yet. Suddenly the sound of rustling hit her ears again, causing her to tense. Reactively, she covered her face with her hands, tears still crawling down her cheeks. The hound emerged from the shadows, dragging a goose along with it by the throat. The white feathers of the creature were stained with blood and there was a lethal wound that had evidently been delivered by an arrow.

This confirmed Ada's fears. She shuddered as the hound dropped the goose to approach her. A wet tongue sloppily left a dog-kiss on her cheek, causing her to snarl out. The hound was relentless – it kept going even when Ada tried to push it away.

"HAWK!" a feminine voice called out. "Off! What are you doing? Is that a woman? Bad boy! Give her some space!"

Ada choked in fear. She hadn't seen another person since being chased by the angry mob from her hometown, and here she was, probably about to be killed by one.

The hound whimpered at the newcomer but darted away from Ada, returning to the goose and bouncing excitedly around his find. Meanwhile, the woman walked closer, her harsh voice shifting to a mercifully soft tone.

"Hello there. I am very sorry about Hawk. You look like you're in need. What is your purpose here?"

When Ada peeked from between her fingers, her eyes settled on a woman with long brown hair and a lightly tanned skin tone. She was dressed in typical hunting clothes: some leathers mixed with cotton garments. Her curious eyes were fixed on Ada as her lips twisted into a frown of concern.

After a minute of silence, the woman spoke again.

"It's alright. I'm not here to hurt you. Something bad must have happened for you to be acting this way."

She got down on her knees next to Ada, rummaged through a burlap sack, and pulled out an apple. Ada's stomach reminded her of just how much she needed that apple as she fixed her gaze on it, unable to look away. Seeing this occur, the kind woman smiled brightly.

"Here," she said, her tone still extremely gentle. "This is for you. It is one of the last ripe apples of the season."

Unable to resist, Ada reached out and accepted the apple. She hungrily buried her teeth into the flesh of the fruit and ate it in several bites. The gnawing in her stomach subsided, if only a little. With that, Ada's blue eyes fixed on the doe-brown ones of the woman who had just fed her. The woman tilted her head.

"My name is Rose," she said. "Who are you?"

Chapter Four

At first, Ada gave no response. She was tense and incoherent. She protested with whimpers, but Rose managed to get her to sit on a tree stump so that she could be inspected.

From there, Rose started to examine Ada's wounds. She lifted up shreds of ragged material and traced her finger over the scars, checking to see if there was any rot. Having found none, she sighed in relief. She raised a brow at the amount of blood that happened to be covering the woman she'd found, but did not ask questions. Her priority was to help.

"You look as though you have been in a battle with *several* hounds and more," she finally said. "No wonder you are wary of Hawk."

The hound perked up at hearing his name. He bounded over but stopped when Rose put her hand up. Despite this, his tail still wagged quickly and with much vigour. Rose shook her head in a stern manner, narrowing her eyes. She instructed him to be calm and then turned her focus back to Ada.

"You need some care," she said in a kind but firm tone. "I've no idea what you've been through, but you won't make it out here on your own – even for another few nights. You look like you haven't eaten in days."

Ada looked down at herself, able to see some of her ribs jutting out from the sorry rags that she used to call clothing. Realising that Rose was both right and without ill intent, she nodded, sniffling a bit. With that, Rose took one of Ada's arms over her shoulder. It wasn't that difficult as they had very little height difference. Then, they began to make their way through a field, heading towards some smoke that was rising into the sky.

When the town came into view, Ada flinched, her eyes widening. Rose took notice of this motion and spoke softly.

"Shhh... I don't know what you've been through but clearly it was horrible. I won't let anyone bother you. We will get you to my home, and then get some food into you."

Prior to heading for home, Rose had collected the goose that Hawk had been holding. The hound walked loyally by her other side, his nose responding to all of the smells of roasting meats and baking breads. His tongue hung out of his jaws, lolling about as his tail wagged happily. Some of the dust from the dirt road coated his fur, causing Rose to glance over and comment.

"I will run the brush through you later, Hawk."

Hawk bounced on his paws as if he understood Rose. Twitching his nose as his claws clicked along the cobblestone, he spotted a bit of meat on the road and hastily rushed over to gobble it up. It had probably been dropped by a food merchant. Ada observed the dog's behaviour, reassured that he was a good-natured one. She still felt afraid of him due to the circumstances though.

They passed several wooden houses painted white. There were beams criss-crossed over one another. The rustic homes had some low fences in front of them, probably for chickens to wander around behind and graze during the day. Currently, none were outside. The town was relatively quiet, but there was some activity here and there where the occasional torch was lit.

When they passed by a particular store, Rose paused to peer inside the glass window. She smiled. There were various pieces of glimmering jewellery on display, showing immaculately shaped gemstones set in various metals. Ada glanced around, still unsure about the situation but slowly calming down. She suddenly felt more at ease to talk to Rose.

"What's this?" she asked.

"My jewellery shop," Rose explained, a hint of pride in her tone. "Why, it demands quite a bit of upkeep. But it's worth it. The wealthy often visit this town and are able to purchase pieces here. The more common gems, just as beautiful, are even sold to regular people here when they are able to afford it. It has taken me over a decade to get to this point."

Ada looked at Rose and realised that the woman was probably in her late twenties or early thirties.

She must have dedicated herself to this from a fairly young age.

Ada nodded, led onwards by Rose through the town until they arrived at a house that was relatively large compared to the others. It was set on a hill, somewhat away from the rest of the townsfolk. Ada wondered if there was a specific reason for this when she spotted a nearby building. It had a large chimney, wooden benches and an overhang consisting of several tools and various hammers. Seeing Ada's interest, Rose explained.

"That is my forge. Men here swallowed their dry insults towards me as a female forgemaster and jewellery maker when they realised the truth – that the quality and care I put into my work far outranks theirs. They had to find business in a different town. I learned only from the best: my father."

Rose stammered over that last part, something that Ada took notice of. Perhaps something had happened to her loved one as well. Now was not the time to ask.

Ada's thoughts were cut short by the rumbling of her stomach. When she reached over and clutched at it, Rose couldn't help but notice.

"Enough about me, dear," she said. "Let us get you inside. I will get you fed."

They entered the home, a warm atmosphere greeting the two of them despite the cold chill outside.

Rose directed Ada to sit down on a comfy chair. It was certainly better than the cave floors she'd been sleeping on. So comfortable in fact, that she found herself starting to relax entirely. Although Ada didn't know this woman well at all, she had been nothing but kind in taking her in. Besides, at the moment, Ada needed to accept all the help she could get.

Rose busied herself preparing the goose; stripping it of its feathers and getting the firepit roaring. Ada was rather close to falling asleep by this point. She willed herself to stay awake though. She'd already had a full day's sleep and it was her weakness influencing her right now – not tiredness. She resolved to watch Rose, noting her muscles rippling as she moved around. It made sense what with her being a hunter and a forgemaster. She had to be strong if she was creating her own jewellery, after all.

Hawk kept his distance from Ada, sensing the fear emanating from the woman every time he went towards her. He shot her a dejected look every so often, but otherwise settled into a pile of furs. He nursed a large femur that had been stripped of its meat. Rose offered him a bowl of goose stew when she had finished making it. She approached Ada with one too, gently handing it to her.

"Are you strong enough to lift the spoon?" she asked.

Ada wasn't sure, but she shakily grabbed it and started to eat. Rose smiled.

"What a silly question on my part," she said. "If you can walk, you can eat. I am merely concerned. I'm glad to see that you are able to eat though. You look so beaten-up. I'll prepare you a bath if you like?"

There was a pause before Ada nodded her head. After another few heartbeats, she spoke.

"Ada."

"What?" Rose asked, furrowing her brow.

"Ada. That is my name. T-thank you," she said finally, a grateful tinge settling into her tone.

Rose's eyes twinkled.

"Ada. What a beautiful name," she said. "Well, it's nice to meet you. The first task will be to get your wounds properly inspected and cleaned up. I have some herbs that will prevent them from going rotten. Even though a lot of your wounds appear to be closed now, a precaution is still better than nothing, yes?"

 Ada nodded appreciatively.

"I saw nothing upon first inspection," Rose added. "But I would like to confirm that."

Satisfied with Ada's response, Rose prepared the tub and warmed the water with a pit below it. Whilst waiting for the water to reach a pleasant temperature, she turned her attention back to Ada. She helped her out of her rags and looked at her wounds again. Ada wasn't shy when it came to this, though she wondered if Rose had yet another talent when it came to health – on top of what she already appeared to know. As if sensing the question hanging in the air, Rose shook her head.

"I am no expert on these matters. We might need to see someone who examines wounds if I find something critical. Though all of this appears to be crusted over with no sign of green, which means we could bypass that if the state of the wounds continues to be clean."

Within moments of Rose having guided her into the bath, Ada sunk into the water. Her muscles truly relaxed for the first time since the angry mob had given chase. The scent of herbs filled her senses, allowing her to close her eyes. She felt a cloth dangle on her arm and reached for it. She kept her eyes closed as she rubbed it over her body. During this, Rose had already gone to clean up after dinner.

Soon enough, there were leaves and sticks floating in the bathwater, along with a few off-colourings from the dirt and blood that had caked Ada's tired body. When she stepped out of the bath, Rose returned to give her a thick cloth blanket to dry off with.

"I don't have an extra bed," Rose said. "But the furniture is very comfortable."

"Your hospitality is enough," Ada replied humbly. "I appreciate it with all of my heart."

"It's my honour, dear. You clearly needed a friend in that wild world. By the way, I am deeply sorry about Hawk's behaviour."

Rose's smile was as sweet as honey. Ada drew in a deep breath, rubbing the bite on her arm. She forced a smile, but inwardly knew that she would need to heal from the damage mentally as well as physically. Her eyes fell upon Rose's hound. He was resting with the bone between his paws, his chest rising and falling peacefully. Ada knew that it would take some doing, but she was starting to feel confident that she would be able to find her strength despite everything that had happened.

"He has a good spirit," she said. "I just need to get used to hounds again."

The first beams of sunlight were beginning to shine in through Rose's windows, prompting a yawn from Ada. Rose took notice of this and directed her to the bed.

"Long night? You must be as nocturnal as the bats at the moment. That is my only explanation as to why you were even somewhat awake during this night. I need a nap as well. You get your rest, and I will set you up in the morning with more food."

Rose had done so much for her already that Ada considered protesting. She decided against it though. The woman clearly wanted to help, and it was needed.

Ada fell into a disturbed sleep, whimpering softly every so often from the nightmares that bombarded her. Surprisingly, a few times during the day's rest, she felt a hand clasp hers. When a nightmare was particularly grisly, she opened her eyes and fixed them on none other than Rose. Her saviour merely wore a soft smile and spoke in a tone to match.

"I can sense the disturbance in your mind. It radiates off of you in waves, Ada. Would you like me to sit here with you for a while? Perhaps it will help. I will have my book on my lap. No one here will hurt you in this little home of mine. Though I barely know you, you are in need. I intend on seeing you get better."

Rose's voice was melodic and sweet – like the siren of legend without the danger. Ada found herself succumbing to it, soothed especially by Rose's humming as she read. It all helped her to get through the day's sleep and eased the pain of her nightmares. Her mind was scarred with what she'd seen, but she was slowly starting to believe that maybe she could get through this.

Rose. Is she a guardian angel?

Ada believed so. She would have struggled to survive if Rose hadn't turned up just in time. The thought didn't haunt her so much as it gave her a beautiful feeling of relief and comfort. Someone was here for her. That was enough to inspire her to keep going.

When should she tell Rose the truth? Certainly not too soon. Thankfully, the woman had not pressed yet, and Ada had a feeling that she wouldn't until the story was ready to be told.

Chapter Five

Something was wrong.

Gasping and clawing at her throat, Ada whimpered. She could feel her lungs filling with smoke. She couldn't get away no matter how hard she tried. Tears ran down her cheeks as the scent of burning flesh filled her nose. She could hear her mother screaming. Her father's death made itself clear in her mind over and over again.

Someone was shaking her by the shoulders. She bucked and let out a cry, trying to shove them away. Whoever it was continued to be persistent though. Soon Ada opened her eyes to fix them upon none other than Rose, who spoke in a soft tone, as if trying to calm a wounded animal.

"It's alright. You're in a safe place, Ada. Please, rest. *Breathe.*"

Ada did as she was told, taking several deep breaths before allowing herself to relax. Upon seeing this, Rose smiled and let out a sigh of relief. Her eyes were full of sympathy and she stepped away to give Ada some space.

"You were screaming in your sleep," Rose said. "Your aura grew darker and darker, filled with fear and agony. I knew I had to do something to stop you from harming yourself further."

"Further?" Ada asked.

She then realised that she could feel a stinging sensation on her palms. She drew her hands in front of her, observing the deep red marks that her nails must have left there. Wincing, she looked back up to Rose.

"Thank you," Ada said breathily.

She sat up, her shoulders slumping in defeat. There were no beams of light shining through the window, indicating that it was nighttime. It had been three days since Rose had taken Ada in. Throughout this time, she had continued to provide food for the wounded woman, keen to help her recover and gain strength. The nightmares had been ongoing though, some worse than others, the worst of them having hit Ada just now.

A bowl of soup was gently placed beside Ada, causing her to rub her head and sigh. Rose remained silent, motioning for her to eat. Ada shakily took a spoon and began to draw it into her mouth. Seeing this, Rose smiled.

"Good," she said. "This will help to calm your aura. A warm belly is helpful in this situation."

Rose sat down for a moment to gently run a hairbrush through Ada's hair, embracing the opportunity to help her relax even more.

"Your hair has a very ethereal look to it," Rose said. "I think it's beautiful. It got so tangled from your "adventures", but I am confident that I can tame it."

At first, Rose's comment had caused Ada to swallow her food uneasily, but she soon realised that Rose had no ill intentions. Hawk, meanwhile, cautiously padded over, looking up towards Ada with big forlorn eyes. Perhaps he could sense the discomfort that radiated from her. She stared at him warily, rubbing at her arm and leaning away from him. Rose cleared her throat and commanded her canine companion.

"You know to leave her be, Hawk," she said gently.

"No, it's alright. He comes from a place of kindness. I need to work on accepting that," Ada admitted.

She shifted her gaze to the dog bite on her arm. Hawk followed her eyes and whimpered, as if detecting the point of contention. Ada hesitantly held out her hand to the hound, causing him to tilt his head and raise his ears. His tail slowly began to wag as he approached, gently sniffing her hand before brushing it with the top of his head. Ada froze during this, but didn't pull her hand away. In fact, she petted him for a few seconds before retracting it.

Happily, Hawk let out an excited yip and bounced over to his bed of furs. Ada smiled shyly, and then looked over to Rose. She had finished trying to tame Ada's hair – for now – and was leaning against the wall, watching the interaction. In a proud tone, she spoke.

"You don't have to do that. But it is brave of you to work on getting over that fear. I can tell by the marks on your arm that hounds must have harmed you considerably."

Ada nodded, shuddering at the memory, but doing her best to push it aside. She gazed around the warm home. The bark-coloured walls were illuminated by the firepit as smoke dispensed from the home via the chimney. The season was only going to grow colder, and bitterly so, but the warmth of the fire allowed everything to be cosier. A shelf full of glittering jewellery was enhanced by the flickering flames. The sparkling reflected in Ada's gaze. Rose followed her stare and chuckled.

"I will show you the forge soon, if you like. Not yet though. You still need to build up your strength. I wouldn't be able to stop myself from asking for little tasks here and there if you were there watching me," Rose said jovially.

She winked at Ada. The two women smiled at each other and it helped to ease the tension from Ada's entire being.

Ada hadn't spoken much since being taken in by Rose, but Rose didn't mind one bit. The jewellery maker had been enjoying herself in telling stories that Ada had listened to happily. Not only did they provide Ada with a pleasant distraction from her very recent past, but she enjoyed the sound of Rose's voice, and just how creative she was at storytelling.

"You must be waiting for another tale, hmm?" Rose began. "Ah! I recall one of a princess – a true princess – visiting my little shop. Normally royals are rather conceited. She was different though. Her scent reminded me of flowers and fields of growing grass. Why, it was as if she had stepped out of a storybook meant for children. Can you believe that she had a little bat on her shoulder? She told me that she had tamed him, and that he was her special friend. She explained to me that her brothers considered her odd for this, but she wasn't bothered. Her mother – the queen of a distant land – had permitted it. I wondered to myself if she *had* stepped right out of a book then. Anyway, she asked me to make her a metallic bat with a sapphire set in the centre of it. I told her that such a piece would take weeks to craft, but she didn't mind. Once I had committed to the job, she turned and walked away into the night. It was late, and she was my last visiting customer. Because she had paid me in advance, I completed the piece without issue. She returned a few weeks later for it, and left a fairly large tip. That bat was still with her! It had an adorable wiggling nose. I don't think Hawk was happy about the scent of it when I got home though."

Rose let out a chuckle, glancing over to a very confused Hawk. The hound was unsure as to why his name had been called, but was happy to be acknowledged all the same.

Ada smiled brightly, taken by the story. She gently tapped the tip of her index finger against her chin. She thought back to her father's ability to shapeshift. Surely that odd visit from the princess had nothing to do with vampires though?

"Maybe there is magic in the world. A tame bat sounds fairly odd though," Ada spoke hesitantly. "Did the princess have any other unusual quirks?"

Rose shook her head and wandered over to grab a broom with which to do some house cleaning. Ada made a mental note to help with that soon. She was gaining strength fast and wanted to give something back – it was the least she could do.

"Her aura was sweet, like edible berries in the forest," Rose continued. "I felt no sense of danger – if that's what you're asking. Other than the bat, and the fact that she was so kind for someone of her status, there was nothing out of the ordinary. She wore darker colours than what most people would: true blacks. She must have had access to *really* expensive dyes. But, well, that is to be expected of royalty."

After a pause, Rose blinked and couldn't help but notice that Ada was hanging on her every word.

"Her aura was somewhat similar to yours, Ada."

Ada rubbed the back of her neck awkwardly. Rose noticed her frown of uncertainty straight away.

"Oh, come now," Rose said. "In a good way!"

The rest of the night was spent exchanging stories. Ada avoided the subject of her parents. Instead, she chose to focus on the happier times in her life, like when she'd explored the forest whilst learning how to hunt.

"It's how I was able to survive out there for so long before you found me," Ada finished, a hint of confidence in her tone.

Rose's eyes sparkled in delight at Ada's words; she even clapped a few times.

"Wonderful. Wonderful! I knew you were a strong woman, Ada. I think being able to sustain oneself is so important. Of course, you already know that from, well…" Rose said, gesturing with her hand and not wanting to elaborate.

Ada let out another soft chuckle, rubbing her cheek gently and pushing herself up. Rose shot her a sharp glance.

"I need to grow stronger," Ada assured. "Sitting here will not aid that. I can do it, Rose. I will do some work as well."

Rose bit her lip cautiously. Holding out a hand, she approached Ada.

"Well, alright," the jeweller said. "On one condition: you allow me to do most of it."

***

A few days later, Ada had gained enough strength and had come out of her shell a bit more to Rose. Although her rescuer only knew tidbits of what had happened, she did not press. Ada would tell her the full story when the time felt right. Even if she would never get to that point, that was alright by Rose. Ada's gratitude and pleasant aura was such that Rose could tell she had a good soul.

Ada had eagerly joined Rose in the forge. Rose happily fuelled the fire and set up her tools. As she approached her materials, she looked over her shoulder.

"Now, pay close attention. You might learn something important! Step one for me is to always…"

The process went on for several hours. Rose – covered in much sweat and grime – managed to create a simple elegant silver band with an emerald set in the centre. She presented it to Ada, who eyed it with much curiosity. She had spent the entire time observing Rose as she'd worked. The jeweller's muscles were strained from the effort. From having worked so hard, her body radiated exhaustion. She was used to it though; when she wasn't hunting or caring for Ada, she worked here in the forge.

Watching Rose made Ada wish that she had put more effort into skill-building over the years.

"You work incredibly hard," she muttered.

Rose shrugged, beaming at her guest.

"I must," she said. "Times tend to be difficult, and my father always taught me to never bend under pressure. Rather, to rise to the occasion and be self-sustaining. In a world where those like me can be seen as lesser, well, I decided to take my life by the reins and steer it along by myself."

Ada's eyes twinkled in adoration as she looked from the forge tools to the woman before her.

"That's wonderful," she finally said, letting out a sigh. "I wish I had done such a thing when I'd had the chance."

"Perhaps you can be my apprentice," Rose said.

Ada stared her down, searching for any signs of jest. Seeing none, she tilted her head.

"Do you mean that?"

"Of course!" Rose replied. "I know a strong spirit when I see one. It'll be nice to have you working with me."

Rose wandered over to pat Ada on the shoulder. The slightest hint of blush spilled across Ada's face.

"I am honoured," she said.

She made a promise to herself that she would tell Rose of her past – and secret – soon. Well, perhaps not *quite* yet; she would grow to help and learn from Rose, and *then* she would tell her.

Why did the thought put Ada's stomach into knots? Surely Rose would not forsake her for what she was? The more Ada thought about it, the more she realised that she was forming a connection with this woman. It made her all the more fearful that she would be rejected for being born a half-vampire.

Chapter Six

A week later, Ada found herself sitting on a hill just a little way away from Rose's home. In the short period of time she'd taken to rebuild her strength, she had gained muscle mass too. There was a "new" gnawing in the pit of her stomach though. She had made an unusually fast recovery and now had the urge to hunt for a different sort of food. To drink blood would be unthinkable though. How would Rose react?

Ada was determined to stick with only the beautiful food that Rose made. She stared up at the stars, raising her index finger to the sky and tracing some of the constellations above. When she heard the rustling of leaves from behind her, she stiffened. She gasped as a hound burst forth. A huge feeling of relief came over her when she realised that the pup was just Hawk.

Knowing that he might have disturbed Ada a bit, the hound danced away from her. He was cautious but still his tail was wagging. He sat a short distance away, his nose twitching as though he could not sit still. He had been letting Ada pet him occasionally even though she continued to display a deep fear of him. He was patient – probably due to Rose's insistence, of course.

Wherever Hawk was, Rose was no doubt soon to follow. Ada waited a moment before hearing footsteps. She smiled as Rose emerged from the shadows. The woman approached and sat down beside Ada. Hawk bounded over to rest his head upon Rose's lap. Rose began to gently run her hand along the hound's head, taking in the night for a moment. She took a deep breath, enjoying how serene the landscape was, and how fresh the air felt.

Both women were dressed in thick furs. A cold breeze cut through the material, causing Ada to shiver a tad. She turned to speak to Rose.

"Are you paying me a visit? Or would you like some help in the forge?"

Truth be told, Ada delighted in helping Rose with her craft. It was the least she could do after the woman had saved her. Rose smiled and shook her head.

"No. I want to sit with you and watch the stars out here. You have your moments of being distant and I like to make sure that you're doing ok. When we return home, I will get the fire going so that we can have some warm tea. How does that sound?"

Feeling comforted, Ada nodded and then turned her attention back to the sky. The scent of winter rushed through the air, some clouds making their way across the stars. An owl flew briefly in front of the moon. Ada wasn't sure what kind of owl it was, but she could hear things that full humans could not; this particular owl was much quieter than other birds – a silent hunter of the night.

As usual, she avoided the subject of *why* she was rather closed off.

"Do you think the snow will come soon?" she asked Rose.

"Yes. You can feel it in the air," Rose replied.

"We'll be ok. I have a strong stock of salted meats in the cupboard. The cold season is always difficult, but it doesn't have to be lonesome."

Ada furrowed her brow, turning to give the kind woman a questioning look. She felt an ache in her stomach. Guilt. She had done little to contribute.

"Are you implying that I could stay here for longer?" Ada asked.

Rose nodded.

"I don't deserve your kindness. Rose, I…"

"Hush," Rose replied softly, her tone a reassuring one. "Before you go on and say you should venture out, that's simply not true. Hawk and I have been incredibly lonesome in the past, and it can be dangerous out here alone. If you seek to leave for other reasons, I understand. But if it is because you are worried about repaying me, please, banish such worries. You can help me with the shop – and in the forge too. How about that? I know you are wary of the town."

Hawk perked up, his tongue lolling out of his

mouth as he tilted his head. Though he had no idea what the conversation was about, he appreciated being mentioned. He wagged his tail as Rose petted him gently on the head, some bits of fur blowing off in the breeze as she did so.

Ada watched this interaction and resolved to work harder on getting used to Hawk. Clearly the two were the best of friends, and Hawk was no monster. Yes, she realised, she would be able to get over this as time went on. She was sure of it. She looked at Rose and smiled.

"It will be lovely to stay with you both," Ada said.

Her voice was firm and confident. She knew that she couldn't let herself be ruled by fear. She had already been through terror, but Rose had made everything alright – even when they had only just met.

"It's about time I did more for you," Ada said. "It might take me a while to feel safe going into town though."

Rose did not pry, her tone merely shifted to one of delight.

"Yes, I understand. In the meantime, you can still join me in the forge. Alright?"

Ada nodded. They chatted for a little while longer, once more telling each other stories. Rose mostly led this, as she always did.

As the sky grew darker, the women stood up to head home. Hawk bounded along with them. Although there were more shadows than light, the women knew their way back (mostly because of Rose). Ada could not help but shiver, her mind wandering back to that forbidden side of herself that she would *never* let Rose see.

"Are you concerned about monsters?" she finally asked.

Rose gave the question a fair bit of thought.

"Monsters and legends," she said softly. "I believe they exist, but I do not fear them. Hawk would let me know if I needed to be wary of someone. He is an excellent judge of character. I am far more afraid of people than monsters, Ada. They get away with things that some monsters could only dream of."

Surprised by Rose's response, Ada relaxed into silence as they walked back home, unable to disagree with the sentiment. The journey was uneventful. Not even the sound of bugs or other animals could be heard. The cold season was indeed upon them, and many had shut themselves away for it.

When they arrived back home, Ada helped with some of the housework. Rose fed Hawk and then got to work on skinning a pigeon for dinner. Some root vegetables were tossed into the pot, a staple of what they would be using to survive the winter. It reminded Ada of the winters she'd spent with her family before the mob had taken them away from her.

After dinner, Rose bid Ada a goodnight. Left alone with her thoughts, the half-vampire could not shake Rose's words. If people could be just as bad as monsters, wouldn't that make *them* monsters as well? What made vampires *worse*? She was aware of her father's crimes, and of how he had turned his life around. That didn't mean that *all* vampires were tyrants (or indeed reformed ones) though. It *couldn't*. Should she be more accepting of the side of herself that she could not deny? Especially since *she* could not be blamed for what her father had done in his past?

***

Another few weeks had passed, and the two women were growing closer. They shared furs more often now, and Ada's stories were finally becoming more fleshed out. She was comfortable with talking about her parents, though the implication that they were no longer around weighed heavily in the air. Still, Rose did not push.

Today, Rose approached Hawk, patting him on the top of the head.

"Be a good boy. I will bring you back a treat if you are."

She offered him an elk bone to chew on. He accepted it, evidently delighted. Ada took a deep breath and moved to approach the hound. Rose shot her a curious – but kind – look.

I can handle this, Ada told herself. As she got closer to Hawk, he tilted his head inquisitively. Bracing herself, she opened her arms wide. The hound looked from Rose to Ada before standing.

He abandoned his bone and trotted over to Ada. He sniffed her arm exactly where the bite mark was. It caused Ada to wince.

He licked the area gently before pushing his head into her abdomen for a cuddle. Ada was tense at first but she eventually managed to relax. She let out a joyous giggle as Hawk yelped happily, licking her on the cheek. His tail was wagging practically as fast as a fly's wings!

Rose clapped her hands and danced around delightedly.

"Ada, I am so proud of you," she said. "I know you were incredibly wounded by hounds. But it means so much to me that you have finally accepted Hawk."

Ada stood up, allowing the hound to return to his bone. She turned to Rose and placed a gentle hand on her shoulder.

"I wouldn't have been able to do that without you, Rose."

"Can I give you a hug?" Rose asked.

After a confirming nod from Ada, Rose opened her arms wide. As the two women held each other, they both closed their eyes. Ada could feel Rose's excited heartbeat. It was almost a bit too tantalising. In fact, her scent was more comforting than any stew they'd had recently (not to put down Rose's cooking, of course). Ada felt her canines sharpen just slightly, but then realised the escalating issue.

She pulled away quickly, letting out a gasp. Startled and hurt, Rose stumbled back. She didn't want Ada to feel guilty though, so quickly decided to focus on something else.

"We should get moving. If there's anything you want to talk about, let me know. Otherwise, let us walk and discuss our plans for the day, shall we?"

Gulping, Ada opened her mouth to say something, but thought better of it. She didn't know how to explain herself, and the heavy feeling in her stomach was growing stronger. She shoved her worries to the back of her mind and made her way into town with Rose, telling herself that she would be just fine. She had to be if she was ever going to heal.

The midday sun blazed above as they walked along the dirt path. The tension eased as they discussed the weather, and jewellery sales. Ada helped by carrying the jewellery in a chest, her exceptional strength aiding in that respect. When they got to the shop, Rose taught Ada how to set up the displays.

Although Ada remained introverted to start off with, she slowly eased up. Once more, Rose complemented her on finding the strength to face her fears. A few excellent sales were made before Rose closed up shop at dusk. They wanted to get back home before dark.

"You did well today," Rose praised.

Ada still couldn't take her mind away from their interaction that had happened earlier in the day. She merely nodded, staring at the ground as they walked. Rose gently placed a hand on Ada's shoulder. Ada jumped and turned to look at her.

"Don't worry about what happened earlier," Rose said. "I'm not upset. Ok?"

Having to accept that, Ada nodded, and they continued their journey home. Once there, first on the agenda was a warm dinner. It helped satisfy Ada, but only for the most part. She couldn't take her mind away from how Rose's heartbeat had felt; so full of emotion, so full of yearning, so full of *blood*.

Even so, the evening went by without complication, as did the next few days. That was until, unfortunately, the fateful night when Ada had remained home to do some cleaning while Rose tended to the shop. For that night, just around the time when Rose was due home, Ada scented blood. The scent was confirmed when the door swung open, and in stumbled Rose.

Her thick furs were stained with blood. Swaying a little as she removed them, it revealed the stab wounds on her arms. Ada's jaw dropped as she could only watch Rose limp to the comfy chair and collapse.

"Ada, oh Ada," she uttered. "They went for the jewellery, but I got away... just barely..."

Chapter Seven

Ada moved quickly to get some cloth strips from a nearby chest. She brought them over to Rose and started wrapping the woman's wounds.

"Thank goodness you escaped," Ada said.

She led Rose to the bed. Whimpering loudly, Hawk charged over. His tail was tucked between his legs, and his ears were drawn back in panic. The tawny fur of his scruff was raised, and his nose was twitching frantically. He inspected Rose whilst Ada rushed into the other room.

Ada grabbed a bucket and ran outside to the well, determined to get some water with which to clean Rose's wounds. It would be clean enough for its intended use. A cold breeze caressed her cheek as she reached over the side of the well. A *plop!* indicated that the bucket had reached its destination. As Ada pulled the rope upwards, she was relieved that the water hadn't frozen over yet. It probably would fairly soon though.

With the task completed, she began to make her way back towards the house. Suddenly, she could hear an animal screaming loudly.

Hawk!

She ran inside the house just in time to see Hawk limping. There was blood trickling down his leg from a gash just above it. It had been caused, no doubt, by an intruder.

Ada's eyes focused on the man. He had pale skin and rotten teeth. She could smell his rancid breath even though he was several metres away. His bloodshot eyes flittered around until he moved his focus over to her. Ada placed the bucket down as quickly as possible and straightened up to face him.

He had greasy dirty hair. It had possibly been blonde at one point but was so caked that the colour had probably changed. His chipped nails were covered in mud, with flecks of blood from his recent actions coating them. He was dressed in rags, and his voice was gritty and laced with exhaustion.

His eyes darted again from a snarling Hawk back to Ada, who tensed up and narrowed her gaze.

"I will get the riches," he said aggressively. "This *whore* doesn't deserve any of it! I will butcher that ruddy dog. And *you,* harlot."

In his hand was a sharp knife. It was already bloody – probably with a mixture from Hawk and Rose. This man wasn't just interested in the jewellery. It was clear that he wanted to loot the *entire* house, and harm anyone who might try to stop him.

This thief thought he could do whatever he liked. Ada had a feeling that he'd ambushed Rose. In a blaze of red-hot anger, the half-vampire's teeth started to show from her twisted scowl. Ever so slowly did the brilliant blue of her eyes bleed into a bright red as her nails lengthened into claws.

Hawk stood there and barked threateningly at the thief. In doing so, he ignored Ada, who was very clearly turning into a monster.

Rose had weakly wandered from the bed to lean on the doorframe, keen to observe what was going on. She had been edging towards the kitchen, probably to grab a knife for backup.

The thief fastened his bloodshot eyes upon Ada, his jaw dropping. He pointed a disgusting finger towards her and screamed.

"DEMON!"

Rather than running away, he made the mistake of lunging towards Ada. She had seen his type before. Having seen her parents murdered in front of her and not having been able to protect them, she would not let her new friends – and saviours – die in the same way.

At lightning-fast speed she was upon the man, fangs sinking into his neck as she pulled up and ripped a few chunks from him. Agonising screams filled the house as she raised her claws and slashed them across his face, ripping out an eye in the process. Blood spurted from him, covering Ada. No matter how disgusting this cockroach was, to Ada, this was *food*.

She buried her fangs into his throat. Drinking to scratch that *itch* that she'd had since she'd started to recover, she felt revitalised. The size of her pupils grew to cover even the red of her eyes, taking over entirely. She was in a *frenzy*, and truthfully, she was enjoying it.

The muffled sounds of Hawk's barking met her ears, but that wasn't her priority in the moment. She eventually let go of the man. He continued to thrash beneath her like a wounded animal. She locked eyes with Hawk, who tilted his head and barked at her.

Her chest heaved as she watched the hound lunge for the man's neck. Hawk ripped into his throat and opened the wounds wider, eventually finishing him off entirely. Covered in blood – some of it his own – he limped away from the man and made his way towards Rose. She was shuddering and leaning against the table in a state of shock.

For a brief moment, Ada's life was bliss. She revelled in the bloodshed. It filled her with ecstasy to see that the man who'd threatened Rose was dead.

That feeling faded when she widened her eyes and realised what her friend had just witnessed.

Now she knows I'm a monster.

Ada stood up and saw the sadness in Rose's eyes. Tears began to pour from her own as she darted towards the door, shaking her head.

"I'm sorry, Rose. I'm so sorry."

Ada felt so ashamed. Just as she was about to make a run for it, a soft voice stopped her.

"Please wait, Ada. Don't go. I need you," Rose begged, her voice dripping with agony.

Ada realised that by running away, she would be abandoning the very person who'd saved her life not too long ago. Not only that, but Rose didn't *want* her to leave. Swallowing her fear, Ada faltered and turned. She rushed over to Rose, who collapsed against her.

"Please. Take me to the bed," Rose said wearily. "Don't leave me. I would like some stew. Can you get me some?"

There was no fear in her voice, just deep sadness, pain, and concern. Was it for Ada?

The half-vampire did as she was asked. The whole situation felt so surreal. She directed Rose to the bed, wincing every so often but putting on a brave face.

Ada was like a ghost gliding along. She cleaned and dressed Rose's wounds and then did the same for Hawk, who was sent to rest on his own bed. He was on his best behaviour, whining at Ada as if telling her to please take care of Rose. Obliging, Ada fetched Rose some stew as requested. She then left her to eat. There were other things to take care of.

She dragged the thief's body outside, carrying a shovel along with which to bury him. The deed only took about an hour; her bloodlust had enhanced her strength. She had considered leaving the body out to rot, but decided against it – at the very least she didn't want to attract too much attention from the wildlife. Plus, despite what this disgusting *thing* had done to her saviour, she would feel the slightest tinge of guilt if she abandoned all of her ethics.

When she returned to the house, she grabbed a bowl of stew and sat down to eat. She was keen to keep her mind away from the inevitable. She heard Rose clear her throat from the other room and hesitated, but eventually made her way to the woman.

"How are you feeling?" Ada asked.

Rose rubbed at one of the stab wounds on her arm and considered Ada's question. After a pause, she replied.

"I feel better now that I've eaten. I wouldn't have survived without you. I hope you understand that."

Rose smiled as she met Ada's normal gaze. It was as if Ada had never shown the other side of herself.

"The thief entered my shop while brandishing a knife," Rose explained. "Some brave customers chased him away. When I thanked them, they assured me that he was a beggar who often attempted to bully his way into getting what he wanted. I thought nothing of it, and turned my attention back to the shop. I underestimated him; he followed me home. He ambushed me on the road, but I managed to fight him off. I obtained many wounds though, as you can see. Without your help when he broke into the house, I would have been done for. Hawk couldn't have taken him on without you."

Ada nodded, a deep frown of hatred plastered on her face throughout the entire story. Rose took notice and spoke softly.

"You're a hero, Ada. Please give me a smile. Why don't you read us a story? Pick one from my shelf over there. It will help us both relax. Join me here. If you are in the right mind for it, I would enjoy the company."

"You want me to rest with you?"

"Would I ask if not, dear?" Rose chuckled. "Light some candles. I am eager to hear you read to me."

Everything still felt so surreal but Ada did as she was told, settling in bed next to Rose. She opened a book on her lap so that she could read to the woman. Rose fell asleep early into the night but Ada remained awake. She decided to pick up a different book to save the other one to read with Rose.

Whilst Ada was keen to lose herself in a book, in the back of her mind, she knew that she would need to have a proper talk with Rose. She swore to herself that she would bring it up – once and for all – tomorrow. It would be disrespectful to Rose to keep on avoiding the subject. The least that Ada could do was to be honest with her – especially after everything they had been through together. Rose had been so patient with her, and clearly appreciated the company.

Ada realised that telling Rose the truth about her identity might not be as horrible as the anxious feeling in her stomach was suggesting.

Chapter Eight

The sun shone through the window as Ada worked to clean up the mess from the previous night. She frowned as the images of her attack on the thief danced across her mind.

Rose rubbed at her wounds every so often. She smiled sheepishly when she noticed that Ada was watching. She knew she needed to leave her skin alone in order for it to heal. It was easier said than done though.

Just like Rose, Hawk wasn't acting unusual around Ada either. The happy hound cuddled up to the half-vampire when she took a small break to rest. She was no longer afraid of him, but was surprised that he hadn't taken a dislike to her now that her secret was out.

It started to dawn on Ada that maybe Hawk had known what she was when he'd first found her. If so, it surprised her that he hadn't attacked her in view of that alone. Rose had mentioned that Hawk would always let her know if there was someone with malicious intent in her presence. Perhaps some hounds didn't hate all vampires, and judged them on the merit of their aura – and actions – instead.

Ada turned her focus back to the cleaning. The silence between the two women was heavy – like an uncomfortable fog. The tension in the room could be cut with a knife. Rose's kind smile fell into a worried frown the more Ada worked. This was not helped by the fact that every muscle in Ada's body was practically rigid; she was dreading the conversation that would inevitably happen. In fact, she was terrified. Everything came to a standstill when she finally spoke.

"I suppose I should explain myself."

She turned to face Rose, taking in the woman's beautiful features and admiring her for a moment. She was so brave, so strong – something that Ada feared she herself could never be. Rose stood up and brushed a strand of hair away from Ada's face. Her glimmering brown eyes mimicked the gentle smile she wore.

"Please don't feel pressured," she assured in a soft tone. "We can talk about this when you are ready – no sooner."

Ada gulped and nodded. Out of respect to Rose, she couldn't avoid the issue – it wouldn't be fair to do so. Hawk bounded over and sat next to Rose, bumping her hand with his head and giving her no choice but to pet him.

"I am ready now," said Ada. "It's time that we addressed this. May we sit?"

The two women sat down together on a large chair. Ada grabbed a nearby fur and pulled it over her lap, running her fingers through it nervously. It was from an elk that had provided an abundance of meat last season, so Rose had said.

"I'm a monster," said Ada.

Rose frowned, seemingly in disappointment. She didn't interject though; she wanted to listen.

"A half-vampire," Ada continued. "My father was a tyrant in his past. He changed his ways, and settled down with my mother. They thought they were safe in the town they settled in. The people somehow found out though. They were baying for revenge and… and…"

Tears began to pour down Ada's cheeks. She buried her head in her hands, shaking with sobs. The memories began to flood back as she told the story. She was clearly haunted by them.

Rose gently rested her hand on Ada's shoulder. When she moved it down to rub at her back, Ada peeked from between her fingers. She was surprised to discover that Rose's expression was one of concern rather than hatred.

"I don't agree with you," Rose finally said.

Confused by Rose's response, Ada cautiously moved her hands from her face, tears still pouring down her cheeks. Rose was now smiling at her reassuringly. Hawk wagged his tail, mirroring his owner's energy. He perked his ears and tilted his head, his tongue lolling out in a friendly manner.

"What do you mean?" Ada asked.

She sensed that Rose wasn't about to elaborate, and would probably want some time to think things through. Much to her surprise though, Rose chuckled kindly.

"You're not a monster," she said firmly. "At least, that's what I've ascertained so far. Have you ever slain anyone aside from the fellow last night?"

"Yes," Ada admitted, now avoiding Rose's gaze. "The… the townsfolk were trying to dismember me. I saw them m-murder my family in cold blood, burning the house down in the process. When they chased me, I... I snapped. I felt I had no choice. I ripped the throat out of a man who was trying to kill me. I'm sure you understand what I mean… I slaughtered him. I had to."

Ada's tone was laced with shame. Her shoulders began to slump. At the time, she hadn't felt guilty. He deserved to die, or so she'd thought. But now, she was not so sure. The rubbing on her back did not stop as Rose continued to try and comfort her.

"It sounds to me as though he deserved it," Rose said bluntly. "You were defending yourself. You shouldn't fault yourself for that."

Ada winced and then turned to look at Rose, locking eyes with her. Slowly, she opened her mouth in a worried scowl, this time allowing her fangs to extend. She focused on the thumping of Rose's heart along with the sweet delicate scent of the blood rushing through her veins. This was something that Ada had needed to ignore before: since she'd met Rose, and up until the incident with the intruder last night, the half-vampire had become extremely skilled in denying her hunger.

Now though, she was distinctly aware of *what* she was, and of the hunger itself. She was disgusted with herself. Amazed, Rose stopped moving her hand on Ada's back. She did not retract it though.

"*I* would fault me," Ada said. "This is what I am. My reasons were not strictly for self-defence. I have this… hunger. I am able to sustain myself on human food – for the most part – but drinking *from* a human gives me more power. It feels both wrong and right. A purely *selfish* endeavour… Of course it was a factor when I attacked the intruder last night. My heart is not pure, Rose. You would be right to send me away forever."

There was a long pause. Rose withdrew her hand from Ada's back. The human woman looked at Ada curiously, and finally just gave a nod. Ada's heart sank, for there was even a part of her that had hoped Rose wouldn't be so forgiving. At least that way, they could get any confrontation over and done with.

Rose put her hand on Ada's shoulder and gave it a friendly squeeze.

"I understand," she said. "There were some selfish reasons at play. What I do *not* understand though, is why I would be right to send you away. Do we not consume for selfish reasons? Do I not gain wealth for selfish reasons? Ada, sometimes life is selfish. Sometimes, it's *ok* to be selfish. You killed two men that the world would be better off without. It's irrelevant that some of your motives were self-serving. You didn't murder the innocent. You killed those *deserving* of it for *justified* reasons."

Shock crossed Ada's features, her eyes widening and her breath catching. This was not what she'd expected Rose to say at all. Truth be told, it all made sense but it still didn't justify her *existence*.

"It doesn't change what I am," Ada mumbled.

"It doesn't," Rose confirmed. "And I am very confused as to why it matters. I am a human, and I feel no despair for it. Hawk feels no despair for being a hound. A bat feels no despair for being born with flight! You saved my life. Without you, I would probably be dead. The books paint vampires as purely monsters. You make vampires look like heroes. I would say there is a variety, therefore, wouldn't you?"

Having heard his name, Hawk jumped up. As he wagged his tail, he did a few twirls and bounced on his paws. The hound could feel the joy and relief rising within Ada, and it was affecting him wholeheartedly. He barked excitedly as he brushed up against Ada's hand for a fuss. The half-vampire chuckled and obliged. It was nice to no longer be afraid of Hawk.

Ada took a deep breath and closed her eyes. All of the stress that had been building up inside of her had been far darker than the reality of the outcome. She had assumed that Rose would be chasing her out with a broom. Thankfully, that hadn't been the case at all.

With a look of intense concern on her face, Rose shuffled closer to Ada. She rested her forehead against the half-vampire's for a moment, gazing intently into her eyes.

"I want you to do something for me," Rose said plainly.

"What is it?" Ada asked nervously.

"I want you to love yourself like I love you."

Ada gasped in surprise. The smile in Rose's eyes did not fade. The two women gave each other a hearty hug and held on for a moment before Ada pulled away.

"I can't thank you enough for being so understanding," she said. "The least I can do is get back to cleaning up after last night. Now though, I will be doing it with a spring in my step rather than a weight on my shoulders."

Rose wrinkled her nose for just a moment, a pout forming on her lips.

"I do wish I could help," she said. "You need to rest as well. After everything you've been through, the least I can do is…"

"You were attacked," Ada reminded her. "Rest. Please. I will take care of things."

***

The sun had set a few hours ago. Hawk had kept Ada company whilst she'd finished the chores. It was a welcome distraction from the whirlwind of her thoughts. She was looking forward to getting some rest but wanted to check on Rose first.

"Is there anything else that you'd like me to do?" she asked.

Rose had a book open on her lap. She peered up at Ada, shaking her head.

"You've done plenty already. Come here and relax with me. I can tell that, despite our discussion, your aura is off-kilter."

Ada thought back to Rose's talks about auras. She had never thought as deeply about them before. Still, she slipped into bed with Rose. Wrapping herself up warm under the furs, she closed her eyes for a moment, her story coming back and overwhelming her. Rose pulled her closer, giving her hair a gentle stroke.

"I can sense your turmoil. It's healthy to let everything out, Ada. You should tell me more about your past. Tell me about some of your favourite and least favourite memories with your family. That will help your mind to heal."

Ada was hesitant at first, but in reality, she knew Rose was right. As she told Rose more about her life, tears fell down her cheeks. She couldn't help but interrupt herself with sobs. The memories, no matter how small, were painful in view of her loss.

Rose reached up and wiped away the half-vampire's tears every so often, her smile remaining caring, calm, and gentle. Into the night did Ada talk, soon drifting off to sleep in Rose's arms. Rose herself, still recovering from her wounds, faded as well. Snuggling up against Ada, she let out a blissful sigh.

Hawk curled up at the end of the bed, no doubt absorbing the calm happy energy and allowing it to relax him.

All was peaceful as they slept a night uninterrupted by nightmares, calmed by one another's presence.

Chapter Nine

Several moons later, Ada was working hard in the forge. The training with Rose had gone wonderfully. She was praised as an excellent apprentice, but with much to learn. The warm season was upon them, promising an abundance of food relatively soon. Rose's recovery was somewhat rocky, but luckily, her wounds hadn't festered. She was back to working at full strength now.

Neither woman had bothered to alert the town of the thief. No one seemed to ask after him or miss him at all; either he had just been passing through or was someone fairly forgettable. Ada had a worry in the back of her mind that the mob who had butchered her family would come for her here. There had been no sign of that so far but she would never allow the concern to fade from her mind entirely.

For now though, Ada's focus was on her work. The scent of burning metal wafted through the forge as she hammered a sword. It was crude and misshapen, but was good practice all the same. A retired forgemaster in town had donated some dulled weapons to her to melt down and craft into something new. Ada had been having lessons with him, as well as with Rose. Rose knew little about weaponry, and her work in the jewellery business had led to connections.

Ada wiped the sweat from her brow as the sun started to sink under the horizon. She smiled to herself, a hint of fang poking out from her lips. She had been allowing that part of herself to show more and more ever since Rose had fully accepted her. The half-vampire began to put her tools away, organising things properly as a warm breeze wafted through the forge. Finally, it was time for her to head back to the house.

Once home, she walked over one of the new fur rugs. They had obtained it from a wolf that had tried to attack Hawk. The hound had fought valiantly, but hadn't been alone. He had managed to get away with a few scratches and bites that had cleaned out well. The wolf hadn't been so lucky, but its meat and bones were utilised for food and tools. Its soft fur also made for a good floor piece.

Hawk was with Rose today. They would both be hungry for dinner upon their return from the shop. Ada delighted in this notion, for she could prepare a good meal for them. She'd been doing it frequently lately so it wouldn't be much of a surprise. She loved seeing the smile that lit up on Rose's face all the same though.

She made her way down to the cellar where the meat was stored. The cold room was ideal for keeping the food fresh. There was a goose that had been caught just yesterday. The meat wouldn't need to be dried or salted – it could be eaten fresh instead. Ada cut off the parts that she wanted to work with and made her way back upstairs. She delighted in applying various herbs and spices to the meat. She was proud of what her mother had taught her in that regard.

The half-vampire felt a pang at the thought of her family. It wasn't as painful as it used to be though. Rose always made a point of encouraging her to think of the good times, and to know that her family fell so that she could live a happy life.

Hating herself was no longer an option, and Ada had come to accept that.

Finishing preparations for the meal, she started the wood stove. Knowing that it would take a while to heat up, she made her way to the bathroom. The warmth of the day was fading, and the cool of the night would ensure that the house couldn't overheat. The chamber pot had been cleaned earlier today and the presence of various fresh flowers aided the quality of the air.

She approached the mirror and before gazing into it, used a bucket of water and a cloth to clean her face. Her hair, as pale as bleached bone, spilled down her back. Her skin was almost that colour as well. Even though her flesh was marked with various bruises and scratches from work, the bites from the aggressive hounds had never truly faded.

Her brilliantly bright eyes shifted to a deep crimson in the soft candlelight. She smiled, flashing her fangs to herself again. She stood up straight and puffed her chest out proudly.

"I am Ada Tepez," she said. "My status as a half-vampire does not make me corrupt. It does not make me evil. I am a beautiful person, and I will be here for those who I love."

"I agree," said a voice from behind her.

When Ada whirled around to see that Rose was stood watching her, she could feel her cheeks going bright red. She hadn't realised that her lover had come home. Chuckling, Rose shook her head, a warm beautiful smile spreading across her face.

"I apologise," said Rose. "I didn't mean to disturb you. I heard you were in here, so left you to it. I couldn't help hearing your remarks as I was passing by though. I just had to jump in as well. Forgive me."

"There is nothing to forgive," assured Ada.

She walked up to Rose and cupped her cheek. The two shared a tender kiss for several seconds. Rose ran her fingers through Ada's hair. Then, she pulled away for a few breaths, moving to rest her chin on the half-vampire's shoulder.

"Thank you for setting up the stove. We will eat well tonight. I have something I would like to give you before dinner."

Surprised, Ada blinked but nodded. She bent down to pet Hawk on the head as he bounded up to her with excitement.

Ada curiously made her way to their room. She sat on the edge of the bed to wait. Rose put her work supplies for the shop on the table before joining her. There was a small box in her hand which she handed over.

Furrowing her brow, Ada accepted the box. As she opened it, she gasped in delight. She reached in and delicately pulled out a sparkling silver chain. Attached to it was a metal piece in the shape of a bat. The bat had ruby eyes, gleaming as if staring up at Ada. The half-vampire brought the piece of jewellery up close to her chest. She couldn't help but feel tearful. Sniffling, she smiled when she looked at Rose.

"This is wonderful. You didn't have to give me this."

Rose shook her head and laughed playfully. There was a twinkle in her eyes and she was overjoyed that her lover was pleased with the gift.

"Of course I did," the jeweller said. "I wanted to show you how proud I am that you finally love yourself."

Rose opened her arms, and Ada embraced her in a warm hug.

"You can have a bite, you know," she whispered into Ada's ear. "I don't mind."

Ada tensed, pulling away and shaking her head. She ran her hand gently through Rose's hair, her breath catching at how beautiful her lover was.

"I don't want to hurt you, Rose. I love you."

In a state of bliss, Rose allowed her eyes to partially close.

"I love you too, Ada. You described that gnawing feeling to me a few moons ago. I want to help with that. You might not think that you need your powers, but they might help both of us when times are difficult. Please. Let me help you. It will be alright. You have the control to pull away when you finish."

Biting her lip, Ada nodded, finally giving in. She nuzzled into Rose's neck, kissing the flesh a few times. She could detect the woman's pulse. It triggered the gnawing feeling that she'd worked so hard to ignore for so long. In this moment, it started up again in a ravenous fashion. Her delicate fangs extended as she slowly sank them into Rose's flesh, the delicious blood of her lover pouring into her like liquid velvet. It felt incredibly nourishing: revitalising.

Ada wrapped her arms around Rose, drinking from her as gently as possible. She was filled with so much warmth before pulling away. Other than feeling somewhat breathless, Rose was just fine. To get her bearings, she put her forehead against Ada's. A soft musical chuckle cascaded from the human woman's lips as she stole a tender kiss from Ada. Once this had concluded, she moved to rest on the bed. It was time to cuddle.

As the two women relaxed on the bed together, Rose cupped Ada's cheek and stared admiringly into her post-bloodlust crimson eyes. The blush in Ada's cheeks displayed a colour that matched. She glanced away shyly, despite how close she felt to Rose.

"Your emotions are growing more and more positive," said Rose. "It makes me so happy. Your aura is less chaotic now."

"You think so?"

"I know so," Rose replied, closing her eyes and allowing her entire body to relax.

The rest of the night – and indeed the warm season – would be one of prosperity, cuddles, and love.

****